Chirp, Cheep, Tweet

With Owen Owl

Written and Illustrated by **VICKI FRIEDMAN**

Year of the Book
135 Glen Avenue
Glen Rock, PA 17327

ISBN: 978-1-64649-148-3

Printed in the United States.

In celebration of
DIVERSITY

Hello my new friend!

I am Owen Owl and I am so pleased to meet you.

I have many bird buddies who want to greet you too!

They can hardly wait to tell you many wonderful things about themselves and each one wants to be your best friend!

Oh my, however will you choose?

They are so excited they are starting to tweet and squawk and screech.

You better turn the page so they will quiet down.

*Bold-faced words appear in the dictionary at the back of the book.

TWEET!
CHIRP
Caw
SQUAWK
HOOT
PEEP
TWEET!
CROW
Cheep
COCK-A-DOODLE-DOO
CLUCK!
Tweet!
SCREECH

Hi! My name is Al Albatross.

I am a **seabird**, which means I spend most of my time flying over the oceans. I am proud to say I have the largest **wingspan** of any living bird – up to eleven feet! Wingspan is the distance from the tip of one wing to the tip of the other. I can do something no other bird can do – I can fly several hundred miles without flapping my wings! I can even sleep while flying. I only go on land to **breed** (make baby albatrosses). I eat fish, crabs and sometimes even follow ships to feed on food that is thrown out.

I think I am very special! Can I be your best friend?

Hello! Bobby Blue Foot Booby here.

Like my buddy Al, I am a seabird that spends most of my time flying over the ocean. About half of us live on the **Galapagos Islands** in the Pacific Ocean. Many people come there to see us and we are friendly toward humans. So I know I can be your favorite friend out of all the other birds in this book! Just look at my magnificent big blue feet! The ladies love them. I have a long pointed bill that helps me catch delicious fish. I am an expert diver and can dive from about 300 feet in the air into the ocean. I can hit the water at 60 miles per hour and can go over 80 feet down into the sea to catch a fish. Isn't that amazing?

I am sure you will agree that I am the most fabulous bird!

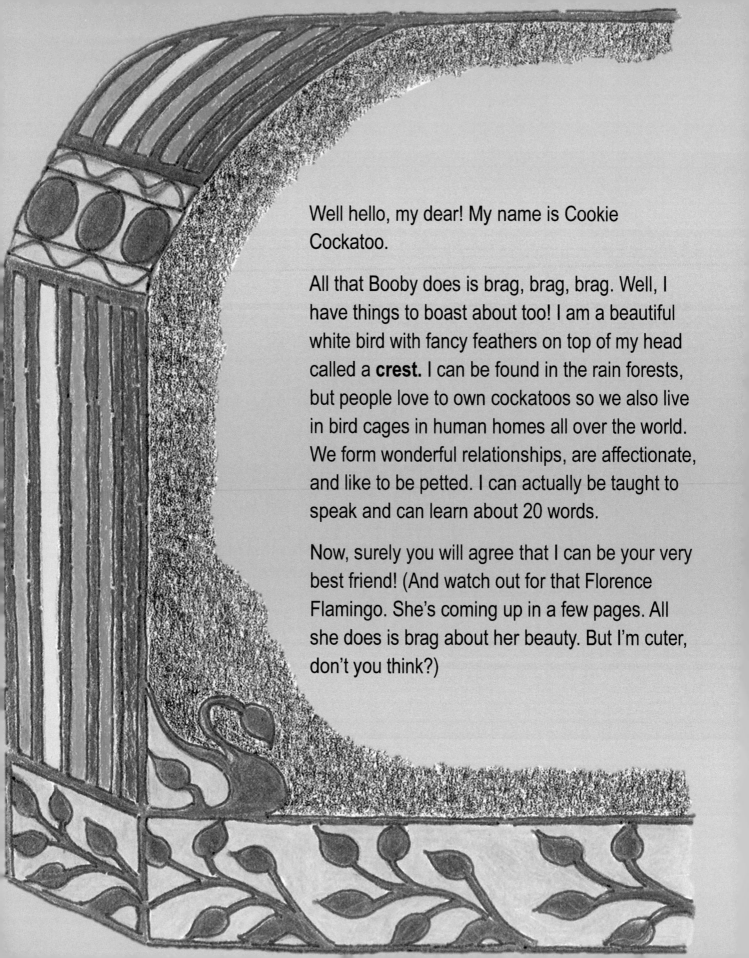

Well hello, my dear! My name is Cookie Cockatoo.

All that Booby does is brag, brag, brag. Well, I have things to boast about too! I am a beautiful white bird with fancy feathers on top of my head called a **crest.** I can be found in the rain forests, but people love to own cockatoos so we also live in bird cages in human homes all over the world. We form wonderful relationships, are affectionate, and like to be petted. I can actually be taught to speak and can learn about 20 words.

Now, surely you will agree that I can be your very best friend! (And watch out for that Florence Flamingo. She's coming up in a few pages. All she does is brag about her beauty. But I'm cuter, don't you think?)

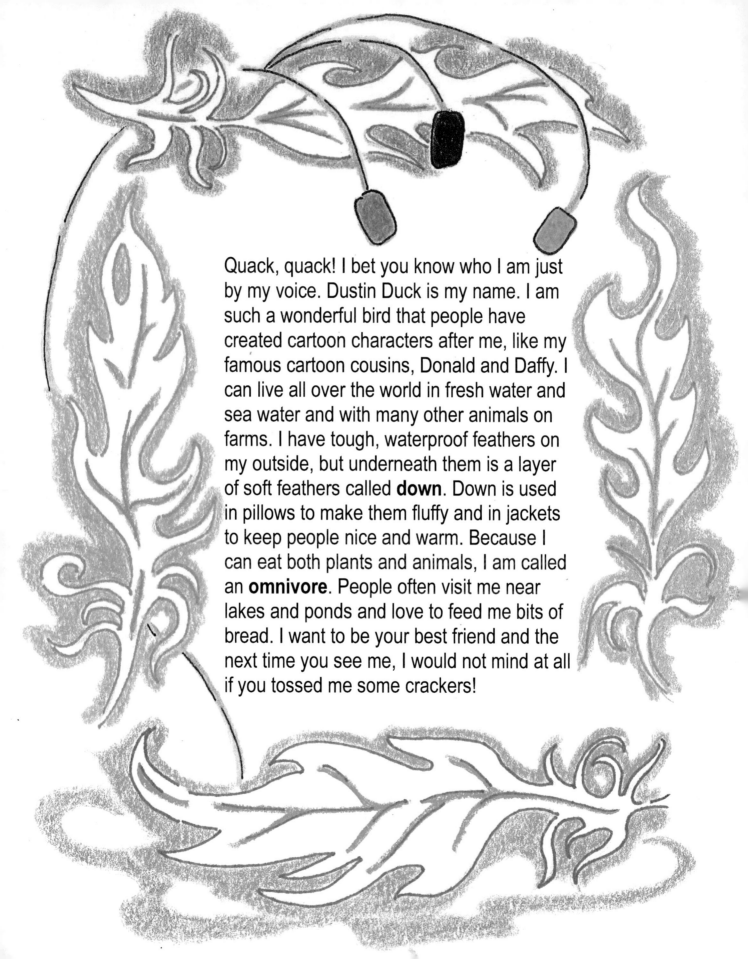

Quack, quack! I bet you know who I am just by my voice. Dustin Duck is my name. I am such a wonderful bird that people have created cartoon characters after me, like my famous cartoon cousins, Donald and Daffy. I can live all over the world in fresh water and sea water and with many other animals on farms. I have tough, waterproof feathers on my outside, but underneath them is a layer of soft feathers called **down**. Down is used in pillows to make them fluffy and in jackets to keep people nice and warm. Because I can eat both plants and animals, I am called an **omnivore**. People often visit me near lakes and ponds and love to feed me bits of bread. I want to be your best friend and the next time you see me, I would not mind at all if you tossed me some crackers!

I am proud to be an Eagle, the symbol of freedom and strength all over the world. You may call me Earl. I am one of the largest birds and have strong muscular legs and powerful **talons.** Talons are sharp hooked claws at the end of bird toes. I also have amazing sight and can see almost 5 times better than a human.

Eagles are **carnivorous,** which means we eat meat and fish. We are also very romantic, as we mate for life. I have one lovely Eagle mate and her name is Edith. We built a huge nest high in a tree where we share the job of taking care of our baby eagles. We keep our nest year after year and fix it up all the time. We are excellent house keepers. Also, I am most honored to say I am the **emblem** of the United States and am known as the king of birds. I am so pleased to meet you and to be your friend!

I'm going to get right to the point and say that I think I am the prettiest bird of all. I am so pretty that people put statues of me on their lawns. Would you believe that there are more statues of me than real birds in the United States? It's true!

My name is Florence Flamingo. My long thin legs, beautiful curved neck and bright pink feathers make me an attraction all over the world. Because people love to look at me, I can be found in many zoos, aquariums and parks.

I bet Cookie Cockatoo is jealous because she thinks she is most beautiful, but I have the beauty category covered! I hold my bent bill upside down to catch food such as little sea plants called **algae,** insects and shrimp. I often stand on one leg and tuck my other leg under my feathers to keep warm. When I travel I fly in a group called a **flock.**

I have so many fabulous things about me that of course you are going to choose me as your most gorgeous best friend!

If you have a bird feeder and see a glorious little yellow bird there, it's probably me!

My name is Gordon Goldfinch and I am small but mighty. I am only about 5 inches long but in the spring my feathers turn a bright golden yellow that makes me stand out from the crowd.

I eat mostly seeds, berries and buds. People love to see goldfinches so they fill their bird feeders with yummy seeds and watch us come to dine.

In the winter, goldfinches **migrate** south to escape the cold weather. We like to live in shrubs and scattered trees. Each state in the United States has a state bird. I am proud to be the state bird of THREE states: Washington, Iowa and New Jersey.

So if you want a special friend, just remember Gordon Goldfinch. I hope to visit you some day... just look for my bright gold feathers!

Get ready, boys and girls, because now you are going to learn about one of the most fascinating birds of all – Me!

Humbert Hummingbird is my name. My friend the goldfinch is small, but I am the smallest bird of all. I weigh less than a nickel! My wings beat so fast that they make a humming noise and that is why I am called a hummingbird. My legs are so tiny that I can't walk or hop. I can only **perch** on a branch. I am also the only bird in the world that can fly up, down, sideways, forward and backward.

I have a long bill and a long forked tongue that I use to suck **nectar** out of flowers. My tongue is so amazing that it can go in and out of a flower over twenty times per second.

I am so interesting to watch that many people hang bird feeders and plant bright colored flowers to attract me to their gardens.

You must agree that I am a special bird and choose me as your favorite friend!

Hi there, y'all! My name is Iris Ibis and I live mostly in the South in warm climates.

I am a **wading** bird, which means that I like to walk in water to catch my food. I can be found in marshes, swamps, lagoons, bays, lakes and rivers.

There are 28 different types of Ibis and we come in many colors. I am a beautiful pure white but many Ibises are red orange, brown, black or grey. (Don't tell Florence or Cookie, but I'm the Southern beauty around here.)

I also have a long neck, long legs, and a large pointed bill. My bill helps me to eat a large variety of things like fish, crabs, frogs, small reptiles, worms and bugs. Don't they all sound just delish?

We live in colonies made up of hundreds of thousands of birds. So if you come down South, be sure to come see me, y'all. I stay with a lot of other Ibises so just ask for Iris!

Abracadabra! Time for a little magic!

My name is Jack Jacana and I can do a special trick that no other bird can do. You see, like Iris Ibis, I am a wading bird and also live in warm climates. However, if you see me, it will look like I am actually walking on the water! How can that be?

I have incredibly long toes and claws that enable me to spread my weight over a large area. I walk on floating plants that are right below or on the surface of the water and so it looks like I am walking on water.

My favorite plant to hop across is the water lily. Also, I pride myself in being one of the best Dads in the bird world. If I see that my babies are in danger from other animals, or heavy rain, I tuck them under my wing and move to another place.

Now, don't you want a magical, good Daddy bird to be your best friend?

Hello! I have a special name that describes what I do best. My name is Kenny Kingfisher. Can you guess why? It is because I am known to be the king of fishing!

We live on the edges of lakes, streams and ponds. I fly over the water or perch on a branch and then swoop down to spear a fish with my sharp pointed bill. I am an expert diver and my beak is as sharp as a dagger. I also have excellent vision so I can see small fish in the water from far away.

There are many kinds of kingfishers but we all have large heads, short legs and stubby tails. In most places we stay where we live and do not migrate South like many other birds. We establish a **territory** and stay inside it.

Now, who wouldn't want to have a king as a best friend?

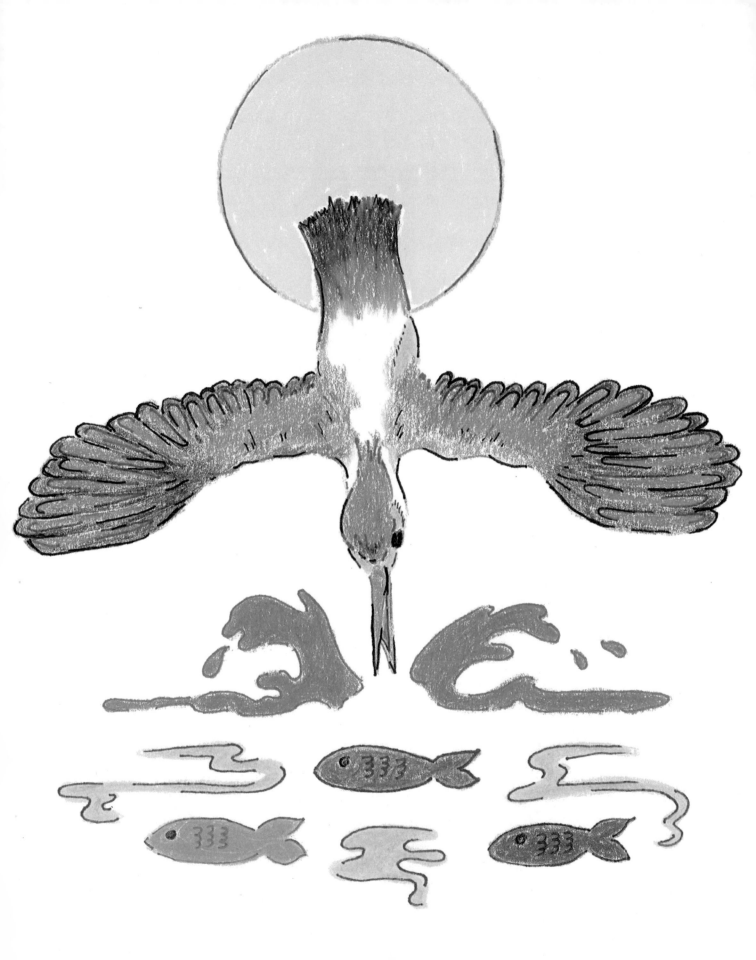

Tweet, chirp, peep, cheep! Do you hear my magnificent voice?

I'm Larry Lark, and I am a songbird. I have such a beautiful voice that when people hear me they feel very happy. That is why people say, "Happy as a lark." I can even sing while I am flying and also have a lot of fun mimicking the sounds of other birds!

I eat seeds and small insects and spend a lot of time on the ground. I even build my nest on the ground. We can be found all over the world and usually live in open areas like **prairies** and fields.

My feathers are mostly shades of brown. I may be little and I do not have bright colors, but I have a voice that is admired by everyone.

I know you would love to hear my glorious singing and want to make me your best friend!

Would you believe that a bird could be one of the most intelligent animals in the world?

Let me introduce myself. I am Maggie Magpie and I must say that I am extremely smart! I can even recognize myself in a mirror. The only other animals that can do that are apes, dolphins and elephants, and of course you brilliant humans.

I like insects, grains, berries, and sometimes I steal other bird eggs as well as leftover food scraps from humans.

Another fact that distinguishes me is that I have a very long tail. In fact, it is almost the same length as my entire body.

Magpies live in many different places like meadows, farms, woodlands and parks. Unlike Cookie Cockatoo, I am a wild bird and am not a good house pet.

There are many types of magpies but we are all large attractive birds with bright colors.

Now who wouldn't want one of the most intelligent birds in the world as a best friend?

Ah, Larry Lark, you have met your match! If you want to hear the most beautiful birdsong then you have to listen to me – Nybert Nightingale!

Many people think that it is the female songbirds that sing, but it is the talented males that show off their voices to attract the ladies. We build our nests in brush just above ground level because we eat mainly ants and small insects that we find on the ground. I have an astonishingly rich range of songs as I can produce about 1000 sounds.

As you can guess, I like to sing a lot at night and that is how I got my name. Like Larry, I am small and plain, with dull brown feathers. But my voice is so wonderful that excellent human singers are said to "sing like a nightingale," and poets use my songs as symbols for love.

Nightingales do not live in America. We live in Europe and when it gets cold we migrate to Africa. So you may not meet me but you can make me your best overseas friend!

Owen Owl here again. Well, I would be remiss if I didn't include myself in this amazing world of birds. Are you having fun learning about this spectacular group of animals?

Here are some neat things about myself. Would you believe that there are about 200 different kinds of owls? We are awake at night and so we are called **nocturnal** birds.

As you know, many bird groups are called flocks. But a group of owls is called a **parliament**. We hunt at night for small animals, insects and fish.

The food that we eat is called **prey**. We have powerful talons that help us catch our prey. We can rotate our necks almost completely around in a circle. Our ears enable us to hear sounds from many directions and our eyes enable us to focus directly on our next meal. As a matter of fact, we are noted to be astonishingly good hunters!

Many of us make a hooting sound for which we are famous. Because we have large eyes and can twist our heads around, many think of us as all-seeing and wise. I am often known as Owen the Wise Old Owl.

I am so glad to be your friend and am thrilled to continue to introduce you to some more fascinating birds. You will have to forgive them for being a little jealous of each other. They are birds after all, and they do like to twitter and gossip a bit. And they all want to be your best friend.

How will you ever decide? Did you notice that I am going down the alphabet? The next letter, then, would be "P." Meet Pete Peacock and Penny Pea Hen.

Have you ever seen such magnificent **plumage**? I'm Pete Peacock and my spectacular tail feathers are collected all over the world. My feathers can be almost six feet long and have the most beautiful colors and patterns.

The picture below is my wife, Penny. She is called a pea hen, and our babies are called pea chicks. A family is called a **bevy**.

We decided to introduce ourselves as a couple because we demonstrate how the male bird often has more outstanding feathers than the female bird. Her feathers are mostly brown in color and she is smaller than I am. I can spread my tail into a beautiful fan shape to attract Penny, but also to make me look bigger and stronger if I feel threatened.

We can be found in the rainforests of many countries, and then many of us are often taken to zoos and parks.

Penny and I are omnivores. We eat many types of plants, flower petals, insects and small reptiles.

We are certain you would love to have such spectacular birds as your friends. If you come to see me, I will give you a tail feather!

Quentin Quail here, hello! I am most popular for being a **game bird**. Game birds are hunted for sport or food.

There are many different types of quail but generally we are small and plump and can be found on all the continents. Most of us weigh less than a pound and have brown and grey feathers that help us hide from **predators**. Predators are animals that hunt other animals for food. I can't blame them—we are delicious!

Humans often eat quail too. Quail eggs are also a delicacy for many animals such as raccoons and snakes.

A distinguishing feature is a group of feathers on top of our heads called a **plume**.

We are **vegetarian** in that we eat mostly berries, grains and seeds and love to **forage** for food in woodlands, forest areas, or brushy deserts.

We build grassy nests on the ground and do not fly very often. So if you want to brag about a bird friend that is very popular and very delicious, just brag about me, Quentin Quail!

Cock-a-doodle-doo!! Can you guess who I am by my world renowned wake up crow in the morning? You guessed right—my name is Robbie Rooster. I am a male chicken and the female chicken is called a hen. Pleased to meet you!

Actually, although we have been crowing in the morning on farms for over 5000 years, we also like to crow many times during the day. I'm a handsome fellow if I say so myself. On top of my head is a bright red crown with points, and right beneath my chin there is another red dangly part called a **wattle**. My feathers come in beautiful colors. To attract hens I do a little dance called **tidbitting** where I shake my head and show off my crown and my wattle.

I am an omnivore as I eat seeds, insects, small mice and lizards. Not only am I good looking, I'm also intelligent. I can remember over 100 different faces of people or animals. Roosters also use over 30 different sounds to communicate to each other.

Did you know that there are more chickens than any other bird? That is because chickens are prized as they provide meat and eggs for people all over the world.

Now, Quentin Quail thinks he is the best tasting bird. I think I am much better tasting. So if you would like the most good looking, tasty bird for your best friend, choose me!

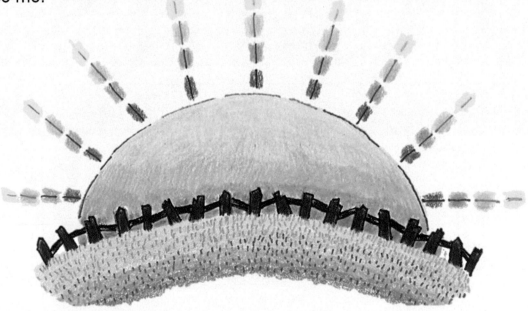

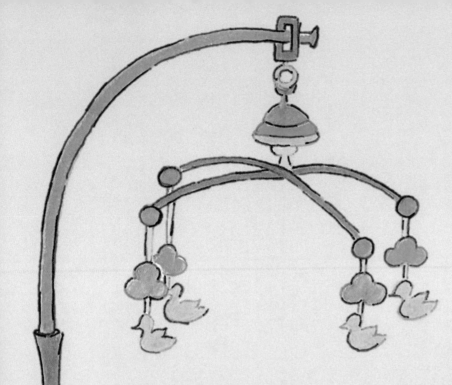

There is a story about me that I carry babies to their mothers. Can you guess who I am? My name is Stella Stork. I really don't carry babies in my beak but I am famous in that I have that reputation all over the world.

Storks are wading birds that live in swamps and **wetlands** in warm tropical areas like Florida, South America and Africa. I have a long, deep bill that I use to catch fish, frogs and other small animals. I am large and heavy with long legs and a long neck.

Storks make huge nests that can be nine feet wide or larger! We build them on trees, roofs, and even the top of telephone poles, and we use our nests for many years.

We can't sing the way most birds do, but we can hiss, screech and clatter our bills together. People think I am very graceful in flight as I soar in the air with my neck stretched out and my legs dangling behind me.

How many bird friends do you know that have a popular story like me? None, I bet. I hope I can be your most favorite friend!

Many of the friends you have met so far have unique features. Bobby Blue Foot Booby has big blue feet. Gordon Goldfinch has a golden yellow chest. Florence Flamingo has bright pink feathers and long legs. Pete Peacock has fantastic tail feathers, just to name a few. But I think I have the most wonderful feature of all. My name is Tommy Toucan and I have a huge beak!

My big, colorful bill is the largest in the bird world in relation to body size. I use it to reach for fruit on the tips of branches and to help me eat small insects and reptiles.

Toucans are usually found in the forests of South America. Because we spend most of our time in trees looking for delicious fruits, we are often found hopping around branches rather than flying in the air.

There are forty different types of toucans, but all of us have jet black bodies and magnificent colored beaks, making us quite remarkable.

We are playful, intelligent, beautiful birds. I am so pleased to get to know you!

Okay, Tommy Toucan. You think you have a special feature? Well, I think mine is extra special. You see, I have an umbrella on top of my head! My name is Umberto Umbrella Bird and the crest feathers on my head fan out to form a cool umbrella shape. No other bird has this famous crown.

I also have a wattle, just like Robbie Rooster, but mine is bigger. I use my wattle to make loud noises.

I live in the **canopy**, which is the tree tops, in the rainforests of South America. Just like Tommy, I hop from branch to branch looking for insects, fruits and berries.

It certainly does rain a lot in the rain forest, but I really don't use my umbrella feathers to protect me. I use them to show off for the gals.

We are relatively large and most of us have all black feathers. Quite dashing, I think.

Now who wouldn't want a bird with a built in umbrella as a best friend?

My name is Vinnie Vulture. I have to say that most of us are unattractive birds. We have brown feathers, sharp hooked beaks and very sharp talons. We are big birds with a wide wingspan. However, we perform a very special function in the animal world. We are nature's clean-up crew.

You see, my friend, we eat animals that have died in the wild. Without us, these animals would rot and smell and the world would be a pretty stinky place. By clearing away the **carcasses** of dead animals we help prevent the spread of diseases such as rabies and tuberculosis.

My head and neck have no feathers so I can stay clean while eating the rotten meat. I also have a very strong system so I don't get sick from my diet. Most of what I eat is actually the bones of the animals so I have strong acids in my stomach that help me digest everything.

We are sociable and like to be with each other. We are **scavengers** that circle in the air looking for food. When we fly, we can go to incredible heights that other birds cannot reach.

As I am an extremely important bird to the world, you can be proud to have a vulture as a friend!

Tap, tap, tap, tap. If you see a dashing white, black and red bird tapping at a tree, it's probably me!! I'm Willie Woodpecker. You may know my famous cartoon cousin, Woody. Indeed, I am one amazing bird!

There are about 180 kinds of woodpeckers and we live in all kinds of places like forests, deserts, jungles and cities. You may see one in your own back yard because we like to visit bird feeders and nest in bird houses. I like to sit on the side of a tree and tap perfectly round holes into the bark and wood. Then I use my long tongue to help me reach the bugs and sap that are inside. My toes and my tail help me balance and grip the trees as I peck on the wood. Woodpeckers chirp and chatter but our specialty is the music we make with our bills! We can drum on objects such as stumps, hollow trees, logs, metal roofing, trash cans and any other object that can echo loudly.

I love to do this to establish my territory and communicate with other woodpeckers. Would you believe I can peck up to 20 times per second? Surely, such a talented bird as I am should be your best friend!

Owen Owl here again.

I am having some difficulty in finding common birds beginning with the letters X, Y, and Z. So let's have some fun!

How about if I make up an imaginary bird and you color it in?

Then I will leave the next two pages blank for you to create your own special bird pictures!

Just think of all the parts – beak, wings, feet, tail – and design your own unique birds.

Would you like to give them names?

Please color me in!

Create your own bird here – have fun!

Here's another page to draw whatever you like!

I hope you had fun learning about my bird friends.

Each one has something that is special and different, yet they are all birds, flying around on the earth that we share with them. They are just like people – we are all different and special in our own way.

Did you decide on a best friend?

I have an idea! (I am a very wise owl, you know.) Why not make them ALL your best friends? You can love and appreciate ALL of them and all of the things that make each one unique.

Now you have learned from all your new buddies that one of the things that makes the world so wonderful is…

BIRD WORDS

*Diversity—Understanding that each individual is unique
and recognizing and appreciating the individual differences*

Algae—Plant-like organisms that live in oceans, rivers, ponds and lakes, and can be tiny or very large, like seaweed

Bevy —A group or collection of birds

Breed—To produce offspring (baby birds)

Canopy—The top layer of leaves and branches of rainforest trees

Carcass—The dead body of an animal

Carnivorous—Meat eating

Crest—An array of feathers on top of a bird's head

Down—The soft, light and fluffy feathers that are underneath the top layer of feathers on some birds

Emblem—A thing serving as a symbol of a particular quality or concept

Forage—A search over a wide area to obtain food

Flock—A number of birds of the same kind that feed, rest or travel together

Galapagos Islands—A group of islands in the Pacific Ocean famous for wildlife viewing

Game bird—A bird that is hunted for sport or for food

Migrate—To move from one region to another according to the seasons

Nectar—A sugary liquid formed at the base of flower petals

Nocturnal—Happening or active during the night

Omnivore—Animal that eats and survives on both plants and animals

Parliament—A group of owls

Perch—To rest on a branch of a tree

Plumage—The feathers that cover a bird and the pattern, color and arrangement of those feathers

Prairie—A large stretch of flat grassland with very few trees

Predator—An animal that eats other animals

Prey—An animal that is hunted and killed by another for food

Scavenger—An animal that eats other animals or plants that have died

Seabird—A bird that lives most of its life near the sea

Talons—Sharp, hooked nails on a bird's foot

Territory—A certain area that is under the control of someone

Tidbitting—A dance that roosters do in which they make sounds, move their heads up and down, pick up and drop off food, and shake their wattles to attract hens

Vegetarian—A person or animal that does not eat meat

Wading—The act of walking through water

Wattle—A fleshy material under the head and neck of several birds, particularly the rooster

Wetland—Areas where water covers the soil all year or for varying times of the year

Wingspan—The distance between one wingtip to the other wingtip

ABOUT THE AUTHOR / ILLUSTRATOR

Vicki Friedman is an established artist residing in York, PA. Based on her career and personal experiences, she wrote and illustrated a book on caregiving entitled, *The Caregiver In You: Inspirational Thoughts and Artwork,* and is the illustrator of 11 other children's books. Vicki graduated with a Master's Degree in art education. Her first career was as an art teacher in Queens, NY. After a move to PA, she worked at the York JCC in many capacities and then at York Hospital and Olivia's House Grief and Loss Center as a Development Specialist. During all of her career years and after retirement, she continued creating artwork, including a series of pieces entitled *Inspirangels,* based on spreading peaceful, loving and inspirational messages. *Chirp, Cheep, Tweet* is a project dear to her heart, as the text and pictures promote diversity appreciation.

IN HONOR OF...

Lonnie Friedman who makes all things possible.

K.C. Delp, Leslie Delp, and the staff at Olivia's House Grief and Loss Center for Children for their assistance with this book, and for their tireless efforts to heal the hearts of children in grief.

Demi Stevens of Year of the Book for turning author's dreams into realities, and for her outstanding talents in formatting the text and illustrations to create the final rendition of *Chirp, Cheep, Tweet with Owen Owl.*